Witchtrot

Embellishments of an Old Maine Legend

J. D. Demos

Witchtrot: Embellishments of an old Maine Legend

Published by Piscataqua Press
32 Daniel St., Portsmouth NH 03801
www.ppressbooks.com

ISBN: 978-1-950381-48-7

Printed in the United States

Burroughs and the Sheriffs,
by Alfred Rudolph Waud, published in
A Popular History of the United States,
circa 1878

*W*hat follows is an account put to paper in 1801 by my mother that fleshes out all the contours of a weird tale she often told us as children.

In her youth, Mother had been an avid reader of her father's extensive library and as a young adult found employment as a schoolteacher. These factors accounted for her exceptional ability with a pen.

The setting of her story was on an old highway known as the "Way to Wells," in the Upper Parish of Kittery, Maine, known as Berwick, that later had taken on the name Witchtrot Road.

We would cajole her into repeating it many evenings, before a well stoked fire, when we mortals felt the "spirits" were abroad. I discovered this written rendition among the papers of my late parents nearly a year after my dear mother's passing.

The tale that follows is in her own words.

William Peeps

Cambridge, Massachusetts,
December 3rd, 1829.

Elizabeth Blaisdell Peeps

Portsmouth, New Hampshire

$\mathcal{I}$t was summer of the year 1763 when I was sent up from Portsmouth town by Papa and Mama to help tend to my grandmother in her slow decline. Grammie Lord lived with her daughter Mary, my mother's oldest sister, in the still wild frontier lands of Berwick, in the Province of Maine. Mary had never married and continued living with her parents through the departures of her siblings and her father's long bout of the dropsy. She stayed on after the apoplexy that took him in March of 1748.

I being old enough, sixteen at the time, but not essential in a household with three other sisters, was chosen to nurse the old woman until her journey among the living was done.

On the day of my leaving, my father, Caleb Blaisdell, led the family party consisting of my mother, Molly, and my sisters Patience, Amy and

Jane. I followed in the rear with my small brother, Peter. We wended our way on foot though the cobbled grid of Portsmouth's streets in a gentle but chill September drizzle. On the walk to the Puddle Dock from our modest brick and wood home, my father strode in front, head held high, nodding to the few neighbors who were out and about, while he kept up a steady murmur of prayers. We, his flock, followed bearing my baggage along the slick pavement.

Coming to the pier we spied the long, flat-bottomed cargo boat known as a gundalow, its mooring lines straining against the river's swift, inrushing current, its triangular lanteen sail swinging lazily in the light sea breeze. The three crewmen busied themselves loading barrels and crates onto the rain-sheened deck under the watchful eye of their master, John Pettigrew, who threw an occasional gaze skyward to adjudge the weather conditions.

After an abundance of hugs and kisses, and some parting advice from my mother, I and my bags were stowed in the tiny cabin toward the stern. My father handed the boatman six coppers for the fare, kissed my cheek, and bid me behave in a manner befitting my upbringing.

Thus I began the half-day boat and wagon trek from the only home I had known, to live with my country kin for as long as I would be needed.

I cannot pretend that I was not frightened and had not shed many a tear with my family before I departed. I hardly knew the old woman who, to a girl as young as I, seemed quite ancient. She was said to be of a peevish nature, doubtless made worse by her chronic rheumatism and a long life of travails.

Father had promised to visit as often as possible, but I feared the coming months, when deep snow and the half-frozen, fast-moving river would make any trips from my home town nearly impossible.

Many roads in those days were mere tracks through the forest, rough pathways best suited to a mounted rider. In Portsmouth, in the town center where we lived, there were good paving-stone streets, but once across the river and into the hinterlands, travel became more difficult.

The sail took no more than a few hours. The high incoming tide propelled us quickly upriver, by many piers and fishing shacks, until we passed the last of Portsmouth's modest outskirts of earthen-colored farmhouses surrounded by bountiful late-summer patchwork plantings.

As the riverbanks assumed the hoary character of a rich woodland of fir, pine, and hardwoods, the clouds began to break, and sunlight shimmered off the rivulets and eddies of the mighty river. In the building heat, Master John doffed his rainslicker and kindly set a small stool on deck for me to better enjoy the terrain. I removed my shawl and took in the scenery, spying the occasional vulture sweeping the tree line or a heron fishing among the salt-marsh grasses. The gundalow's lee-boards, mid-ship on either side, alternately dipped into the water and rose gracefully as we tacked upriver.

Passing Bloody Point and the mouth to Great Bay, we made way speedily, despite the light winds, far up the Piscataqua and into the mouth of the Salmon Falls River, long ago known as the Newichawannock. A few farms and woodlot clearings, with a laborer or two, greeted my eyes. My ears were alive to the wind and the sound of the hull cutting through water.

By the latter part of the seventeen hundreds, the long series of wars with the French and their Indian allies was over. The attacks of the late sixteen hundreds by marauding Abenaki and French had died down after the French and English treaty of the year 1717. By 1763, the time of my journey, they had become mere morality tales used to frighten the innocent into obeying their elders. The rare sight of a white-bark canoe and its now beggared occupants was also the ideal opportunity for older brothers to spin yarns to terrify their younger siblings. Embellished stories of surprise raids perpetrated by vaguely described painted savages, the axe-splitting of heads, taking of scalps, killing of infants, and the capture of the young and weak had the expected effect on unfledged youngsters.

However, according to the accepted narratives of those times, after long marches through desolate wildlands the Protestant captives faced their worst nightmare by being handed over to Jesuits and their unholy masters. Most were more in fear of the Catholic poison corrupting their loved ones than the heathen brand of spirituality. But, fundamentally, they believed that any soul turned from the True Faith was still one lost to the darkness and torment of the Prince of the Air.

Though I would later come to know the fuller truth, such sinister ideas plagued my young mind as I journeyed into the wilderness borderlands.

The tangled flotsam and jetsam of the riverbank, deadfalls, dense underbrush, and dark forestland stirred ghostly visions of wild men lying in ambush. An exquisite dread pulsed throughout my body.

I was full of such fears as the gundalow turned a bend and a bustling ship landing came into view. A pair of coasters and a few shallops were tied fast to a large wharf of huge pine logs. A dozen men in tattered, loose-fitting breeches and linen shirts struggled to transfer cargos of rum and molasses barrels from the Caribbean and textiles and finished goods from the old world into waiting wagons and carts. Into this activity, I was delivered to the shore.

The sight of a young woman in white petticoats and a close-fitting bodice brought all activity to a halt. Under the rude gaze of the workmen, I dropped my eyes and I fear my cheeks reddened. Master John helped me down the gangway and had me wait with my belongings while he negotiated transportation for the last leg of my journey.

The shipmaster soon returned with a young lad wearing a large-brimmed hat, his clothing dirty and sweat-stained by the heat of the day. He removed his head covering and bowed in greeting.

"I know where you be going," he said. "The old Warren place be but a few miles up the Wells highway and is on my way." A shilling facilitated the loading of my things onto his two-wheeled tumbril, the kind of wagon that one day would transport Marie Antoinette to the guillotine. He helped me to settle on a crude pillow in the back. By now the activity of work had resumed, as the novelty of my arrival had worn off, and we set out as soon as the rest of the boy's goods were loaded.

The highway was but a rutted track - likely a muddy slop in wet weather, but in the dry, hot afternoon that had baked out the earlier rainfall it had become a hard, uneven road. Wide near the landing, it narrowed to a five-foot breadth as we traveled away from the riverine warehouses and into the surrounding farmlands.

Simple houses and barns were scattered along the way. Cows, pigs and children clustered about the dwellings. Women busied themselves with chores, laundry hung luffing in the slight breeze, and all living things suspended their actions momentarily to observe the passing newcomer. A few faint smiles and casual nods greeted me, but most of the faces I encountered were sullen and harried looking.

After an hour's bumpy ride, we came to a corner on the "highway" and turned onto a rude trail leading off to our right. I was later to learn that this was the way to York village. A dirt path led to the front of a one-story, weathered, clapboard-clad house with a loft under its low-pitched shingled roof. My guide reined in his nag and we stopped.

The simple house was about twenty-five feet in length, fifteen wide, and sat upon a fieldstone foundation. Four twelve-pane windows were set either side of the front door and a solid stone chimney rose through the center of the peak, with just a trace of smoke rising from its cap. Four smaller windows graced each end, two on the first floor and two in the gable of the loft.

To the right of the house were a modest-sized barn and a few outbuildings of plain wood siding set directly on the earth. The barn's roof sagged a bit in the middle but appeared sound. Garden plots surrounded the house with fields of various crops stretching out beyond.

From the front entryway emerged my Aunt Mary, wearing a blue striped skirt and muslin blouse and wiping her hands on her red checkered apron. Her head was bare, with her long, graying hair tied in a bun. She smiled slightly at the sight of me and approached the wagon to help me down. "Welcome, child," she said as she accepted a kiss from me on her cheek. "Your gramma been anxious to see you here safe."

My wagon-driver carried my bags to the doorway, and I rewarded him with a tip of two pennies. Climbing back into his cart seat he flicked the reins and the horse and wagon pulled off, leaving a trail of dust.

The interior of the house was simply furnished. A plain but sturdy table and chairs, a pine hutch and a pair of tables near the chimney stove were cluttered with washing and cook pots, storage jars, utensils, and plates. Several chests and a rocking chair completed the contents of the large central room. A rough set of stairs against the center of the back wall led to the upper story and was flanked by two small windows. A small storage room took up the west side of the lower floor, where casks and barrels of staples were stored neatly, and a few plucked chickens hung from hooks on the upper floor joists. All was well swept and dusted. To the east end another, somewhat larger chamber was occupied by a dresser with water pitcher and mug set atop, next to a small bed where, under a comforter, my frail grandmother sat propped up on two pillows.

As I entered, Grammie Ruth, turning at the sound of steps on the old floorboards, smiled broadly and held out her arms in greeting. "My dear," she managed in a soft, hoarse voice, "how I've longed to set my eyes on you." I approached the old woman and planted a kiss on her forehead. "My you have shot up an' become quite a fine looking young woman."

Auntie Mary, entering behind me, spoke. "She been talkin' 'bout nothin' else this past week."

Grammie, her thin white hair sprouting beneath her nightcap, began an attempt to slide off the side of the bed. Mary hurried to stop her. "Now you know you shouldn't get up. You're not well enough." She returned her mother to her place, fluffing up the pillows behind her back.

Grammie gave her a hard look, but acquiesced. "All this fussin' will surely be the death of me," she grumbled.

I sat on the bed and put an arm about her shoulders. "You just rest easy, dear, and let us take care of you."

"Blasted old age!" she blustered. "I've become

completely useless."

Mary smoothed the bedclothes and chastised her mildly, "Now behave. You still got plenty of the devil left in you. Obey doctor's orders and you'll be back on your feet in no time."

I stroked her hair and she turned to me, her gaze softening. "My, you are a fine sight for this broke-down old shell."

"You are as beautiful as always."

"And as crabby, " Mary murmured, too quietly for the aged woman to hear.

"Tell me all about yerself and what you been about these past few years," Grammie Ruth's blue-grey eyes fixed on mine as she relaxed back into her sitting position. "There must be some fine young men competin' for your favor . . ."

I spent an hour with grandmother, bringing her up to date on all the family in Portsmouth and telling her some of the exciting tales carried to our town by the tall ships visiting from the Earth's four corners; about disputes between Whigs and Tories and the rising fever in the land that would soon lead to war with Britain. When she looked tired I left her to rest and Aunt Mary helped me to unpack and move into my sleeping arrangements in the loft.

As the days and weeks passed we settled into a new routine. I took over the household chores, the cooking, and the care of the old woman. This freed up Mary to tend more to her gardens and help the hired man, Thomas, work the modest fields about the old farm and care for its few animals.

The late summer was still hot and, aside from occasional storms, too dry. But the well held out and we got by comfortably. Grammie Ruth did gain back some strength and often managed to make her way to the rocker by the fire to keep me company as I worked. Dressed in her linen nightdress, muslin chemise and nightcap, and bundled in blankets on cool evenings, she chatted on about old times or interrogated me about any town gossip I had picked up from the neighbors on my infrequent trips to the landing for provisions.

It was one evening as darkness fell that Grammie told me the tale of her encounter with the Salem witch. A distant storm flickered, casting frequent light about the interior, as a near-steady rumbling provided an unsettling atmosphere to the story.

I was but a chit of five year or so that night of the third of May 1692. The war with the papists and the Indians was still racking our land and the Candlemas attack that past January at York roused great fear among our people, 'specially we folk who lived in the hinterlands. My father, Peter Warren, and my mother, Mary, lived with we three children in this very house before it was raised from the earth and provided with a proper foundation. There were but a few tiny windows in each wall and the bottom floor was dirt covered in straw.

My father's father, James, had been in the war between Scotland and England, and was taken captive by Tumbledown Dick Cromwell, as my grandfather, Covenanter James, was wont to call him. My grandpa would not speak about the battle, but I heered that it was a frightful bloodbath, killing many thousand Scots, with thousands more made prisoner.

James the Covenanter was forced to come here with many others as indentured laborers to work the sawmills and fell the huge trees that once covered this country. Two other Scots, who had finished their terms and been granted land by the Kittery magistrates, cleared land for farming in the sixteen seventies. Those lots lie on the opposite side of the "Way to Wells" and were the homestalls of Sander Cooper and George Gray. Sander's old home still stands to the north and has been bettered over time. Goodman Gray's old house is the fallen-down wreck you have seen, just eastward. My father bought this piece ten years later.

Sander had been gone many a year by the time this night's ruckus took place, his only son John having got the dwelling and farm. Old George Gray was still alive, living with his wife Sarah, though he be terrible hobbled by growing age.

It was a grim time of ruin and want for the coast towns from New Casco to Boston and on top of it, witch-fever had took hold early in the year about

Salem Village way south o' here. We Berwick folk had heard tales of bewitched children, o'ercome with fits and evil visions, calling out their elders as Satan's doers. A great hubbub of denunciations had took hold like a plague cursing all the people.

That May, a minister, George Burroughs of Wells town, had been charged and orders sent for his arrest and removal to Salem. Early that day of the third, word spread down the highway that the man had been seized and three lawmen were carrying him south through Berwick.

The weather was much like 'tis today, with storms coming from the west. Most skirted our farm to the north and west, but the sky were much perturbed. Father and my two older brothers had gone into town for errands.

With twilight growing mother and I worked the garden plot in front of the house, me with a too-big rake trying to smooth out the clods of dirt from her weed pulling, when four horsemen approached from the east.

The pack was led by a short-legged but broad-shouldered man astride a black mare. Dressed in a rust-colored blouse and black pants, and black leather boots, he wore a long black cloak and black wide-brimmed felt hat. Behind, a tall man clothed in black waistcoat, pants, cape, and tall black hat rode straight-backed and official-looking on a black stallion. He had a long gun perched on his saddle. Two shabbily dressed riders, also holding muskets, followed at the rear on ponies.

A lofty mass of dark cloud rising in the west further dimmed the waning light as an abiding rumbling foretold the coming of a fierce storm.

The first man steered his horse and stopped by we two women as the others come up. He doffed his hat and bent his head politely. His dark eyes fixed us with a sober look. "Good evening, good woman. My name is George Burroughs, minister at Wells. My friends..." he shot a glance back at the others, "...and I could surely use a cup of water."

At that, we all heard a shout, "Ho ye!" and saw the old gadfly, George Gray, bareheaded, hobbling with the aid of his oak cane, crossing the road from his homestall. His boys, Alex and James, and their mother Goody Sarah followed. The tall man in black turned his horse and challenged the old man. "What do ye want, old fellow?" George limped up to the horseman's side and stared up at him.

"The divil a bett," he answered.

"What?" The man in black's expression went quickly from puzzled to fierce. "Be careful with your tongue, old fellow," he pointed his crop at George, "or I'll have ye up before a judge!"

George drew his lips back, showing his yellowed but toothy grin, and said, "Be ye the marshal come to take the preacher a Salem?" He scratched the thin white mane of his head and used his stick to refer to the lead rider.

The gloaming was hastening as clouds darkened the sky. Patches of light flickered behind the black wall of storm with a brattle of distant thunder.

"Aye. I be Marshal Partridge and he be my charge," the rider stated high and mighty-like. Just then a sharp crack of thunder caused his mount to start in fright and his stern look turned to one of disquiet. He peeked back at the coming tempest and added less surely, "But we be in a hurry and there be no time to put up with any of your foolishness."

"Nay, nay," Old George answered. "I only be here to serve, 'tis all." His grin grew broader. Near darkness had fallen.

"Then get us some water, by God, and leave us be!" A sharp gust blew up the brim of his hat and he grabbed at it to keep it from flying away.

As the gathered group began fading to mere shadows, Old George said, "I think ye best take shelter afore ye be scorched by the heavens."

"We ha' no time..." the official began as a searing flash of lightning cut across the sky, chased by a fearful crash of thunder.

Another white-hot burst followed, lit up the land like broad day and revealed to all a moment's sight of the minister and his steed hovering midair. It was a frozen picture of the man holding fast to the reins, his other arm flung high over his head, and the steed arch-backed with its back legs kicking out. As full dark dropped back down, the other horses bucked off their riders, and their guns fell to the ground. We women and children screamed out and ran for our dwellings as a cataclysm of rain fell.

More lightning showed Old George standing his ground still smiling, rainwater pouring off his white pate.

Burroughs got control of his ride as the three constables plucked themselves off the earth and ran to our doorway, slipping and falling on the now muddy ground. Hatless and soaked, the marshal and one of his lads tried entering the door and jammed themselves, shoulder to shoulder, in the opening. "Spread out!" Marshal Partridge barked at the men. All three collapsed through the entryway and landed in a sodden heap on the floor. My mother threw the door shut and ran to my side. The men scuttled like crabs across the floor and we all huddled by the hearth as the storm peaked.

One of the shabby lawmen stuttered to his boss, "Here is another fine pickle you done got us into!" The marshal reached for his hat to swat him, but found it missing.

At that the door flung wide and revealed, in another fierce flash, the silhouette of the clergyman. "Ayeee!" screeched the second deputy as he tried to hide behind his fellows. "He really be a warlock!" Another blast shook the house.

Reverend Burroughs closed and barred the door. He calmly removed his headgear and shook the water off it as he strode over to our quivering clutch. Flashes of light pranced about the room, yet the noise of the thunder seemed to be abating.

The first deputy cried out through chattering teeth, "Lucifer will slay us all afore we can deliver him to justice!" The marshal was struck dumb, staring at Burroughs in wide-eyed terror.

"I have secured our mounts in the barn," the reverend calmly said as he sat himself in the chair by the glowing embers of the fireplace. He took a piece of cordwood and stoked the fire back to life. The lawmen scurried to a corner far away from the man of the cloth.

As the storm noise quieted, the marshal asked timidly, ""Tis true ye can lift a great musket with but one finger in the barrel?"

"Bollocks," grumbled the minister. "I need at least one hand."

"I hear that yer Casco house were haunted and full of toads."

Burroughs smirked. "Nay, but there are toads there in summer."

The thunder by now had slackened, though the lightning still lit the faces of the three fearful constables.

"They say you lift a great barrel of molasses out of a canoe by yerself."

"Ye be a cabbagehead. 'Tis an idiotic lie."

"They testify ye be the head of the witches and do lead them in their Hellish Sabbats."

"Ye fopdoodles!" bellowed Burroughs as he leaped from his chair and charged the men with his fists clenched. The three jumped to their feet and ran to the exit. Throwing up the crossbar, they yanked the door open and fled into the rain. The minister slammed it shut behind them and returned to his seat.

"I be terrible sorry for that outburst, missus," he spoke in a mild tone and then put his head in his hands.

Soon we heard the galloping horses of the constables fleeing the farm.

My mother and I still clung to each other on the

floor trembling in fear. While she hugged my shoulders, I anxiously squeezed my hands, wringing each one like a wet cloth. The clatter of rain on the roof had quieted as the storm passed off east. The fire dimly lit the figure of the minister. His shoulders shook, and we saw he was sobbing. "Why hath God abandoned me?" he choked out.

Mother spoke softly, "The stories of the madness down south been carried to us. Such strange matters hath befallen some in our parts these past ten year but it were clear 'twas the sins of envy and greed that fired the accusers."

The reverend lifted his head and nodded. "I was minister to Salem Village twelve years ago, but that damned..." he held out his hands in a bid for forgiveness. "Pray pardon me."

He sat back in his chair and rested his hands on his legs. "The Putnam family were a powerful force in the village. My wife and our two children lived for some time with John Putnam Senior and after my Hannah died in childbirth I had to borrow money from him for her burial. The village had not paid my full stipend and though Putnam agreed that it was some of the money I was owed, he later tried to collect the debt. I, being hardly able to support my new wife Sarah and children, had to abandon my parish after two years and move back north to Black Point." He sighed heavily and wiped the tears from his eyes.

My fear lifting, I left my mother's soothing grasp and went to his side. He looked to me kindly and stroked my hair as he continued his story.

"You know about the terrible Indian attacks at Falmouth and Black Point in eighty-nine and ninety. The first assault, as well as Sarah's death from cholera, drove my family south to Wells. By God's grace we were able to escape with our lives, not like so many of our brethren. There I married again to my Mary, yet it was still dangerous there, as the strike on York early this year showed."

My mother rose and stood before him listening.

"Then the vile slanders began to crawl about Salem Village and beyond. From small girls and others, it spread like fire in a dry field. Ann, Putnam's granddaughter, was the first one to lay charges on me for bewitching. Her head must have been filled with abhorrent stories of me by her family.

"As Christ Jesus is my savior, I know I be a sinner. Yet I swear that I made no pact with Satan nor be no ringleader of witches. All is folly and slander." His head once again sank into his hands and he let out a great sigh.

"When the constables arrived at my home, I was having supper. Knowing I was innocent, I told my family that I would go voluntarily and would be back as soon as I cleared my name."

Burroughs, all of a sudden, stood up and said, "I must be off to find the marshal." My mother laid her hand gently on his shoulder and responded, "Nay, nay. 'Tis late. Ye should stay the night with us and I'll make us some supper." After a bit of haggling he agreed and we finished the evening in near silence.

At dawn I awoke to the voices of the minister and mother below. Heading down the stairs from my bedroom, rubbing the sleep from my eyes, I found him making his goodbye. He strode outside where he had tied to his saddle the lawmen's muskets picked from the mud.

As he climbed upon his horse, he paused to take her hand and bless her for her succor and kindness. Then, tipping his hat to us, he trotted away on the still soggy ground. We saw him turn onto the path to Newichawannock and watched until he disappeared over a rise.

A week later we learned from townsfolk that the constables had somehow found their way to the landing late the previous evening. When Reverend Burroughs arrived that morning, he returned their guns and they, with their spunk renewed, took him once more into custody.

Months later the final sad chapter of the Salem witch frenzy reached us in Berwick. On August nineteenth of 1692, the poisonous accusations, trials, and executions neared their peak when poor Burroughs was hanged along with four others. This madness would not fade until late in that year when the government, finally waking from the lunacy, put an end to it all. But not 'til they had stole the lives of twenty-five innocents, most women.

And it were too late for poor George Burroughs, the only ordained servant of God who died. It was told that, with the rope about his neck, he recited the Lord's Prayer perfectly, something not thought possible for a disciple of the divil. It started a near riot among the onlookers who threatened to stop the killing, but the hangman kicked out the stool aneath him and the Reverend were turned off.

Postscript

*S*uch is the account of Grandmother Ruth on her brush with the supposed ringleader of the Salem Witches. I have tried to faithfully reconstruct her story based on notes I jotted down shortly after her first telling and later questions I made to her about details.

I nursed Grammie until her peaceful passing on the evening of twelve September. Her final decline had been swift after a long period of moderate health, yet her mind was quick up until the end.

A few days afterward many relatives - Warrens, Lords, Neals, Hurds, and my parents - joined on her last journey to the Warren plot by the Salmon Falls River in Berwick town. Her husband long dead, she wished to lie with her parents and grandparents on the old farmland first tended by James the Covenanter.

The day was gray overcast; air still and dry. The world held its breath as we loaded her simple casket into a wagon and headed to town. The only pronounced sounds were the horse's hoofs clip-clopping on the dry road and the squeakings and clunks of the rude hearse. Birds, long past their courtings and nestings, provided her a solemn elegy of late-summer cooings and whistlings. Somewhere in the wood a large woodpecker tapped out a military drumroll accompanied by the sweet flutings of a wood thrush.

In those days payment for a cut headstone was beyond most people's reach. Grammie's spot, like those of her kin, is marked with a simple field stone once turned up by ancestral plows.

*M*any years later I was to study much of the history of the Salem witch trials.

Reverend George Burroughs died on August the nineteenth, sixteen ninety-two, along with four others, including John Proctor. Proctor's wife Elizabeth had been one of the first five women accused of witchcraft early in the year. She escaped execution that day only because she was with child.

The well-off Proctors, tavern keepers, had been caught up in the hysteria when, in the beginning of March, Ann Putnam Junior, granddaughter of Burroughs' enemy John Putnam, charged that Elizabeth's specter had choked, bitten, and pinched her, and she had seen her "amongst the witches."

Ann had been one of the first who became "sadly Afflicted of they know not what Distempers," according to Reverend John Hale of nearby Beverly, who attended to the first two stricken young girls in the household of Mr. Samuel Parris.

"These Children were bitten and pinched by invisible agents; their arms, necks and backs turned this way and that way, and returned back again, so as it was impossible for them to do of themselves, and beyond the power of any Epileptick Fits, or natural Disease to effect, Sometimes they were taken dumb, their mouths stopped, their throats choked, limbs wracked and tormented so as might move a heart of stone, to sympathize with them, with bowels of compassion for them."

After several weeks a local doctor declared them tortured by an "Evil Hand." Hale agreed that they were bewitched.

Thus, the madness began.

The Proctors' maidservant, Mary, later testified at a public hearing that one evening she had seen a shadowy shape she thought was Goody Corey, one of the so-called witches. As the ghostly figure drifted past, Mary snatched and pulled it toward her only to find that the specter had changed into the shape of her master, John.

The month before his hanging, John Proctor wrote a letter to officials in Boston to protest the innocence of those who had been imprisoned. In it he stated that five of his cellmates, all confessed witches, had lied. "Two of the five are...Young-men, who would not confess any thing till they tyed them Neck and Heels till the Blood was ready to come out of their Noses..."

These cruelties, and the fact that the accused were forced to face withering prosecution without an advocate are stains that will not be removed for generations. Worse still, the magistrates allowed the public as well as the "afflicted" to attend the hearings to harangue the poor women and men charged with witchcraft.

Yet it was the reliance upon "spectral evidence," in our times barred from courtrooms, that so startles a modern person. The following document from the Massachusetts Supreme Judicial Court records was accepted as proof of George Burroughs' guilt. I have carefully copied the original, including its odd English vocabulary, punctuation, and spellings:

"[August 3, 1692]

The Deposition of Ann putnam: who testifieth and saith that on 20'th of April 1692 :at evening she saw the Apperishtion of a Minister at which she was greviously affrighted and cried out oh dreadfull: dreadfull here is a minister com:what are Ministers wicthes to: whence com you and What is your name for I will complaine of:you tho you be A minister: if you be a wizzard; and Immediatly I was tortored by him being Racked and all most choaked by him: and he tempted me to write in his book which I Refused with loud out cries and said I would not writ in his book tho he tore me al to peaces but tould him that it was a dreadfull thing: that he which was a Minister that should teach children to feare God should com to perswad poor creatures to give their souls to the divill: oh. dreadfull tell me your name that I may know who you are: then againe he tortored me & urged me to writ in his book: which I Refused: and then presently he tould me that his name was George Burroughs and that he had had three wives: and that he had bewitched the Two first of them to death: and that he kiled Mist. Lawson because she was so unwilling to goe from the village and also killed Mr Lawsons child because he went to the eastward with Sir Edmon and preached soe; to the souldiers and that he had bewicthed a grate many souldiers to death at the eastword, when Sir Edmon was their. and that he had made Abigail Hobbs a wicth and: severall wicthes more: and he has continewed ever sence; by times tempting me to write in his book and greviously tortoring me by beating pinching and almost choaking me severall times a day and he also tould me that he was above wicth for he was a conjurer"

The witch trials and executions continued until after the last court session in September of 1692. Seven more of the convicted were put to death on the twenty-second of that month.

Days earlier an eighth, Giles Corey, who had pleaded "not guilty" but refused to answer any other questions, was pressed to death by the loading of heavy stones on his chest. In the midst of his torment he is said to have responded when asked if he was ready to talk by simply saying, "More stones." The life was slowly crushed out of him after nearly two days of agony.

After seventeen months the hysteria had waned and William Phips, the new Governor in Massachusetts, alarmed at the excesses and worried that the proceedings had violated English law, suspended the court actions on May of sixteen ninety-three. What was likely a greater motivator was that his own wife was about to be charged as a witch.

It was suggested at the time, by those of a sensible state of mind, that if Satan had truly bewitched citizens of the colony it was not the accused, but the accusers and the others swept up in the delirium who had been led astray.

Elizabeth Peeps

1801

Author's Note

This is a rendition of a legend long told in my part of Maine, concerning the origin of the modern name of Witchtrot Road, now in South Berwick and York, Maine. Sarah Orne Jewett, the 19th century author, related a version of the tale in her 1894 magazine article, *The Old Town of Berwick.*

I have tried to adhere to the historical facts concerning the Salem witch trials and the physical descriptions of what was once part of Old Kittery, Maine, and the surrounding region. I have described the inhabitants' dress, housing, transportation modes, and language as best I can.

However, I have taken liberties with the creation of a fictitious family and a Warren home set on the old highway to Wells. And other persons, although historical, have been embellished for the story. As to the core of the legend here told, I have shamelessly ad-libbed.

John D. Demos

South Berwick, Maine, 2020

Acknowledgements

Thanks to Wendy Pirsig and Norma Keim for help with historical details. And to Jane Orr for her patient editing and suggestions.

www.ingramcontent.com/pod-product-compliance
Lightning Source LLC
Chambersburg PA
CBHW032113170626
46808CB00008B/3044